It's your kisses in the morning
when you wake up with the dawn,
getting ready for a new day
with a stretch and a yawn.

It's spending time together.
It's watching clouds float by.

It's saying 'sorry' when we're wrong . . .

and 'well done' when we try.

It's smiling at a stranger.

It's giving friends a hug.

It's cuddling up out of the rain,
warm and dry and snug.

It's helping one another.
It's trying to be kind.

It's waiting for a buddy
when they get left behind.

It's playing and it's talking.
It's laughter and it's fun.
It's heading home together
when the day is done.

It's all these little things
that make you such a special you.